The Vanishing Mouse TRICK

Rose Impey

Illustrated by Peter Kavanagh

Hodder
Children's
Books

a division of Hodder Headline Limited

To Felicity, who sadly found the mouse

Text copyright © 2000 by Rose Impey
Illustrations copyright © 2000 by Peter Kavanagh

First published in Great Britain in 2000
by Hodder Children's Books

The rights of Rose Impey and Peter Kavanagh to be identified as the Author and
Illustrator of the Work respectively have been asserted by them in accordance with the
Copyright, Designs and Patents Act 1988.

10 9 8 7 6 5 4 3 2 1

A Catalogue record for this book is available from the British Library.

ISBN 0340 78514 4

Printed and bound in Great Britain by
Richard Clay Ltd, Bungay, Suffolk

Hodder Children's Books
A Division of Hodder Headline Limited
338 Euston Road
London NW1 3BH

The
Vanishing Mouse
TRICK

About the Author

Rose Impey lives in Leicester, where she was
a teacher for some years, before she started
writing. She still spends a lot of time in schools
talking about her work or testing out new stories.
Rose has written over sixty books for young
readers. Many, like *The Vanishing Mouse Trick*,
are based on her own experiences.

Chapter One

I think I should level with you from the beginning – this isn't one of those girl-longs-for-pet, girl-gets-pet sort of stories. I'm not like Kerry; I don't sit gooey-eyed in front of Pet Rescue. I'm not really into animals. So when Minnie first moved in, I didn't think, oooh, a little mouse, how cute. I thought, oh great! Something else for me to sort out.

*

It all started on Monday morning. Mum was in her usual state of crisis. My mum isn't a morning sort of person. She doesn't really engage her brain until she's had her eleven o'clock coffee break. So, even though she was already running late, she was eating her toast and bleaching the sink at the same time. Mum works in a hospital. She's got this thing about *germs*.

I was eating a second bowl of Crunchy Nut Cornflakes and trying to line up the packet so I didn't have to watch my brother Ned – who's nearly fourteen, spotty, with long legs and big feet – eating with his mouth open.

Suddenly Mum starts up, "What d'you think these little black bits are?"

"What black bits?" grunts my brother, letting loose a spray of Coco Pops.

See what I mean?

"These," she says. I go over for a closer look. "I cleared some up yesterday, and the day before, but here they are again."

There are two or three small collections of tiny black seed-like things dotted along the worktop.

I guess straightaway what they are but I say, "Probably tea leaves."

This fools no one because we use tea bags.

"Probably mice," says my brother and I just want to brain him.

Mum drops the cloth and her face goes white. This is what happens. The smallest thing panics her.

"Mice!" she screams as if one has just run up her leg. "Go and ring Dad."

There doesn't seem much point since Dad's living a hundred miles away and by now will be on his way to work.

"He'll already have left," I remind her.

"We might catch him . . ." she says, racing to the phone. And she does. Even though Dad's also running late he stops and talks to her for quarter of an hour, trying to calm her down. Soon we're all going to be late.

Not many things bother me, but being late is a capital offence at my school. Mr Wade, our headteacher, has a thing about *punct-u-ality*. So I stand leaning against the front door, in my coat, with my bag over my shoulder, sighing heavily. But Mum fails to take the hint.

My brother's sitting on the bottom stair practising card tricks. He spreads the cards into a fan and holds them out to me. "Take one," he says, "any one you like, but don't let me see it."

I roll my eyes and groan. He knows I want nothing to do with his stupid magic tricks. But Mum's still holding forth and we aren't going anywhere, so I take one. I show him it's the Ace of Spades.

"I said, *don't show me*!" He snatches it back.

Just then, Mum pushes the phone towards me – "Dad wants to talk to you." I almost drop it when she squeals, "God, look at the time!" as if *we've* been keeping *her* waiting. She runs upstairs, scattering my brother's cards in all directions.

"Why does he never want to talk to me?" Ned complains.

"He's got taste," I tell him and turn my back on him. "Hi, Dad," I say.

"Hi, Micks. Mum sounds a bit upset." I think to myself, tell me something I don't know. "Are you sure it's a mouse?"

"Looks like it."

"Well, do you think you can sort it?"

I'm tempted to ask, why me? But when I turn and look at the Neanderthal sitting on the stairs pulling pretend cigarettes out of his ear and making them disappear them up his sleeve, I know the answer. "Okay. I'll try."

"You're a little star," he says, which makes me sort of glow like one. "I'll be home Friday teatime. Just keep it out of Mum's way until then. Get rid of the evidence, you know."

"Yeah, yeah." I think I can do that.

"Of course, if you can catch it, even better."

"Catch it!" I shriek. "How?"

I know Dad's late for work. I can hear him rattling his keys. "Oh Michaela, just use your . . ."

"Okay," I say, putting down the phone before he can say the dreaded word: *initiative.* He's always telling me to use it, ever since I can remember. "I hate that word!" I snarl.

"Temper, temper," says my brother. And he pulls a bunch of paper flowers from under his arm

10

and offers me them with a stupid grin on his face. I stare at them, wondering whether they would actually fit up his nose when Mum comes racing downstairs screaming at us to *get in the car!* – as if we've been holding her up.

Sometimes I wonder what other people's families are like. They can't all be like mine. The whole world can't be mad, can it?

A few minutes later I was sitting in the car thinking about what I'd just told Dad I'd do and not having a clue where to start. Mum was sitting hunched forward over the driving wheel as if this might move the traffic along a bit faster. She was muttering to herself, "A mouse! That's all I need on a Monday morning. Ugh! Just think of the germs!"

I turned to the back seat and gave my brother a see-what-you've-started-now look.

"It probably wasn't a mouse at all," I told her. "Even if it was, it may never come back. And if it does I'll take care of it." I put my hand on her arm, like Dad does, and said, "You do the driving, I'll do the worrying."

She smiled at me, letting out the breath she'd been holding on to. But the minute we turned into the High Street and the traffic was even worse, she started up again.

"We're going to be late. We're definitely going to be late."

A voice from the back seat said, "Hey, Pud, look at this."

I turned to my brother and glared at him. That was my baby name and definitely not suitable for a person going on eleven and he knows it. He was laying a pack of cards up and down his sleeve so they rippled backwards and forwards. He'd been practising and he was getting good at it but I wasn't going to tell him that.

"Trick's okay," I said. "Pity about the face."

My brother thinks if you're going to be on TV, *and he is*, your image is as important as the tricks you do. So he practises faces too.

Mum looked into her rearview mirror and asked him, "What's this face supposed to be?"

"Drop dead cool and confident," he said. "What do you think?"

Even Mum managed to laugh.

"Honestly, or not honestly?"

"Honestly brainless," I said. And I gave him a withering look. I can do faces too.

Mum pulled up outside my school and dropped us off. Ned's school's another ten minutes down the road but this is as far as Mum will take us.

When she drove off he opened his hand wide, showing me his empty palm, then he tugged my ear and pulled his dinner money out of it.

"Have a nice day," he said, smiling.

I closed my eyes. "Just go," I said, praying there was no one around watching. Life's hard enough without idiotic older brothers embarrassing you. I took a deep breath, let it out slowly and walked into the playground.

Playground! I don't think so, it's a jungle believe me.

Chapter Two

I walked round the outside of the playground rather than risk picking my way through the yelling mobs in the middle. At the moment everyone in my school seems to be football mad, even the girls. Everyone except me and Kerry, that is. The whistle was just going so I looked round for her. No point. Even though I was late I should have known Kerry would be later. She came racing up at the last minute, puffing and panting. She's useless at getting up in the morning. We both headed into the classroom and sat down.

I don't hate school or anything, but if I had a choice I certainly wouldn't come. Even to see Kerry. It used to be okay, when we had the table to ourselves. Well, apart from Timmy Winkler,

but he doesn't count. He's so quiet you can forget
he's there. But since the new boy came it's just not
the same. Max Grimes is such a pain.

I don't think he likes school much either. He
grumbles all the time about what a waste of time
everything is. I try to ignore him, but he really
gets on my nerves. Look what happened this
morning: I only asked him if he could please be
quiet because he was putting me off my work.
The next minute he jumped up, swept my books
on to the floor and walked all over them. Now
they've each got a big fat footprint on the cover.

The Vanishing Mouse Trick

I didn't bother showing Mrs French; she hates people telling tales. Anyway while he was off making trouble elsewhere, it gave me the chance to have a private conversation with Kerry about the mouse, which was another big mistake. Kerry never does understand how I end up with these major problems to sort out. But then she's got an ordinary family.

I know things will be easier when Dad comes back from Bristol, whenever *that* will be. His firm sent him there because they've been having problems with their new computer system. It's taking weeks to sort out. He's living in a hotel, which he hates. We all hate it, especially Mum, because she relies on Dad for everything. That's why it felt as if the mouse could be the final straw.

When I was younger Mum had a bit of a nervous breakdown. I can't remember it but Dad's always worried it will happen again. So he tries to make sure she doesn't get stressed, because if she does she starts to panic. Sometimes you wouldn't guess she's got this responsible job organising a hospital, but I know that's part of the trouble. By the time she gets home, she's always *exhausted!*

The Vanishing Mouse Trick

So when Dad's not around *someone* has to look after her. Don't ask, what about my brother? He lives on another planet.

So there wasn't anyone else apart from me, was there? But I didn't know how to catch a mouse and I didn't know who else to ask, apart from Kerry.

We were doing maths at the time. Or at least I was. Timmy Winkler was drawing one of his dreadful battles with air strikes and bombs and tiny little bodies blown into pieces with arms and legs flying in all directions and Kerry was drawing hairstyles on the inside cover of her maths book.

I leaned over and started to tell her, "We've got a mouse."

"Oh, how cute. I'd love a mouse."

"I don't mean a pet one!"

And just then Max Grimes came back and sat down.

"We had a mouse once," he said, immediately poking his nose in. "My dad set a trap and it was me that found it. It was horrible. Its poor little eyes were popping out of its head. It was all gungy . . ."

Kerry pressed her hands over her ears. "Tell him to stop," she hissed at me. "I can't bear it."

"She's easily upset," I explained, "if it's anything to do with animals." Actually I didn't feel too great myself imagining a squashed dead mouse. I'd never seen a live mouse close up, never mind a dead one. But I couldn't afford to think about it. I still needed some information.

"So, where would you get a mousetrap," I said, "if you wanted one?"

"Pet shop, of course."

I should have checked Kerry still had her ears covered.

"You wouldn't!" she turned on me.

I looked at her helplessly. "I've got to get rid of it somehow. My mum's freaking."

"How could you, Micky? Mousetraps are instruments of torture. They're cruel and hateful and so is anyone who'd use one. Have you stopped to imagine what it would be like?"

Max Grimes clutched himself around the throat. He made his eyes bulge and a trickle of spit ran down the side of his face. It was a useless impersonation of a dead mouse, but it made Timmy Winkler giggle.

"It's not funny," said Kerry. "Animals have rights too, you know. I'm going to join Animal Liberation when I'm old enough."

"It was only a joke," he snapped at her.

"Some things aren't joking matters," she snapped back at him. "Some people should learn when to keep their stupid jokes to themselves."

I rolled my eyes and wished I'd never brought the subject up.

Max leaned over and put a thick line right through Kerry's drawing. She opened her mouth and stuck her arm up. She soon dropped it though, when she remembered she was supposed to be doing fractions in her maths book, not drawing hairstyles.

"You're horrible," I said, knowing he wouldn't risk scribbling on my maths work. He pulled a disgusting face at me instead. "You want to be careful you don't stick like that," I told him.

The Vanishing Mouse Trick

Then we sat and stared at each other. But he was the one who looked away first. I could tell people didn't often stand up to Max Grimes, but he didn't scare me.

Chapter Three

Since I have to walk through the precinct on my way home, I decided to call into the pet shop to try to get a mousetrap. Seeing all the cages full of pets, it felt a bit odd coming in to buy something to kill one with, until I reminded myself: mice aren't pets; *mice are pests*. They poo on your worktops. And I saw in a programme on TV that everywhere they go they leave this trail of wee that's invisible to humans so you can't even see where they've been. Talk about Germ City! And I've told you about my mum and germs. Believe me, I didn't like the idea of mousetraps any more than Kerry did, but this mouse had to go.

As soon as I walked in I could tell the man in the pet shop thought I was up to something. He had this suspicious look on his face.

"What do you want?" he said.

"A mousetrap."

"What for?"

I couldn't think what else to say. "To trap a mouse?"

"No need for sarcasm, young lady. Have you got enough money?"

I struggled to keep my temper. How would I know until he told me how much it cost? I opened my purse and showed him my money.

He sniffed. "D'you want to catch it or kill it?"

This felt like a trick question. Surely I needed to do both.

"I just want to get rid of it," I said.

He reached behind him, stuffed the trap into a bag and slid it across the counter. "Ninety-nine pence, please. And don't trap your fingers."

I grabbed the bag and left without waiting for the penny change. I didn't dare ask him how to set it. Perhaps it was already set. I walked home holding the bag at arm's length, as if it had a loaded gun in it.

I was still home before Ned, even though I'd called into the pet shop. I let myself in and went straight through to the kitchen. I got such a shock!

Even though my head was full of the mouse, I didn't expect to walk in on it.

There was a flash, that's all, just a blur and it was gone. Under the dishwasher. My heart was beating as fast as if I'd come in and surprised a burglar. I dropped the bag on the table and stood there trembling. I wasn't scared. I knew it was only a mouse. It was the surprise.

There was a fresh pile of droppings, two or three little piles, in fact. One on top of the tin of drinking chocolate. I collected them all up in a piece of kitchen towel and put them in the bin.

Then I thought about all that wee you couldn't
even see so I cleaned the worktop and everything on it with Jif.

I heard the door open and my brother
came into the kitchen. He was shuffling his
pack of cards. He never goes anywhere
without them. Dad calls them his security
blanket. But Ned says if you want to be a
brilliant magician you need to practise,
practise and practise some more. Believe me,
he does.

"I just saw the mouse," I told him.

"Where?"

"It disappeared under the dishwasher."

Ned knelt down and ran his hands under
the bottom of the door. "There's a big gap,"
he said. He tried to reach underneath but
he got his arm stuck. "It might still be there.
Let's take the door off. I'll get the screwdriver."

That's just the kind of thing he'd do, as
well. And then not be able to get it back on.
And then the dishwasher wouldn't work. And
then Mum would have a fit, etc, etc. You see
why Dad asked *me*?

"Don't be stupid," I said. "It won't still be there. It wouldn't be living under the dishwasher. Anyway I've bought a trap. It's in the bag." Ned picked it up. "Be careful," I warned him. "It might be set."

He held the bag by its corners and carefully tipped the trap out. It landed on the table with a clatter. I must say I was a bit disappointed when I got a proper look at it. It was only a thin bit of wood with a metal spring. It was called *The Little Nipper*.

"I can't see how that's going to work," I said.

"Oh, it's very simple," said Ned, starting one of his little lectures. "Look, it works on a lever principle. You create the tension by drawing back the spring here. Then this prong slips into that loop which pulls the end bit up." He prodded it, tentatively. "The minute the mouse steps on it . . ."

The Vanishing Mouse Trick

BANG! The noise was deafening. The trap flew up in the air and skidded across the table.

Ned swore, really loud, then started sucking his finger. When he took it out of his mouth the tip was bright red. I couldn't help laughing.

"It's all right for you. That blooming well hurt."

"I did warn you," I reminded him. "Run it under the tap."

I could see how it would work now. A little mouse wouldn't stand a chance. I remembered Max Grimes' description. I was beginning to feel sick.

Food was the last thing on my mind. But it takes more than that to put my brother off eating. When he gets in from school, he's like a human vacuum cleaner. He consumes anything in his path.

He sat at the table with a little collection he'd made: grapes, a mini choc-roll, a pickled onion, a few cubes of cheese and a tin of frankfurters. He baited the trap with bits of each, then he tried to steal them back with a pair of kitchen tongs.

I watched in disgust. Such a small mind in such a big head. Each time the trap snapped back it caught the tongs and held on to them for dear life.

But when Ned tried to trip it with the end of a frankfurter and bits of sausage exploded all over the place, he'd gone too far.

"Stop that!" I said. "And you can get it cleaned up, now, before Mum comes home."

"Keep your wig on. It won't look any prettier when the mouse is in it," he told me, grinning.

That was the final straw. I just wanted to murder him.

"You made the mess," I yelled. "You clean it up."

Suddenly we heard Mum's key in the door. I grabbed the trap and hid it in the cupboard under the sink. Ned swept all the mess into the bin. We both sat at the table trying to look as if butter wouldn't melt in our mouths.

When Mum walked in she immediately looked suspicious. "What's going on?"

"Nothing," said my brother.

"We were just wondering what was for tea," I said.

"I've brought pizza. Turn the oven on while I get changed will you? I've had such a day. I'm absolutely . . ."

". . . *exhausted*," Ned and I said together.

Ned got up and followed her upstairs. I could hear him telling her about some friend he'd invited round to practise magic – surprise, surprise!

While she was gone I boiled the kettle and then put the pizza in the oven. When she came in she started looking round the worktops. I knew what she was looking for.

"There's not been a sign," I lied. "I told you, it's gone."

She sat down with the cup of tea I'd made her. I could see her lean back and relax. Like Grandma says, sometimes a little lie is kinder than the truth.

Chapter Four

At seven on the dot the phone rang. I picked it up. "Hi, Dad."

"One of these days," he said, "it won't be me."

"I doubt it." You could set your watch by my dad. He rings every night at seven o'clock for a daily bulletin and, boy, does he get it. Mum curls up on the stairs with a glass of  wine and talks to him for about an hour. She goes through this list of all the things that have gone wrong from the most trivial, like the fact that we've run out of toilet roll, to the more important, like the fact that we've got water coming through the kitchen ceiling every time we have a bath.

She lets me talk to him first though.

"Where's Ned?" Dad asked. Usually I have to race Ned to get to the phone, but tonight he was tucked away upstairs with his new friend, Darren.

"He's got a friend round. Apparently they're both into magic so they've got this idea about a double act."

"Interesting," said Dad.

"Scary," I said. My brother hardly ever brings friends home so Mum's dead pleased because she thinks it's a sign he's normal after all. But it isn't. It's just a sign he's found someone else as weird as he is.

"How are *things*?" Dad dropped to a whisper. As if anyone else could hear!

"Under control," I said. "I bought a trap today."

"Well, be careful you don't trap . . ."

"Yeah, yeah," I said. "That's not the bit I'm worried about."

I couldn't even bear to spell it out, but I didn't need to; Dad guessed.

"Well, supposing you do catch anything – and you probably won't – here's what to do! Leave it in the trap – throw an old tea towel over it, so you don't need to look at it. Make sure you put a pair of rubber gloves on – scoop the whole lot into a carrier bag – tie it up and put it all in the dustbin."

He made it sound so simple: *How to dispose of a body in five easy stages.*

And he made it sound so clinical, calling the mouse *it* all the time.

But what I wanted to know was, how do you *not* look at something? Once you've seen it, you've seen it. And if you've seen it, like Max Grimes had, with its eyes bulging out, and all gungy, how can you *unsee* it?

But I didn't get the chance to say any of that because Mum came down from having a bath, towelling her hair dry. I handed her the phone.

"Have you finished?"

I nodded. "I'm going to watch TV." I needed a bit of light relief.

I closed the door so I didn't have to listen to Mum's day of woe. I curled up on the sofa and flipped channels trying to find something to take my mind off my problems. I found a couple of soaps, which did the trick, until suddenly, something distracted me.

It was such a small movement, not much more than a hair blowing across my face. Out of the corner of my eye I spotted the *mouse* – sitting in the middle of the carpet – cleaning its whiskers!

I hardly dared to breathe in case I frightened it off. I watched its little miniature head turn from side to side, checking out the room. I studied it as if I was on a quiz show and I had a minute to

remember as many things about it as I could.

It was much darker in colour than I'd expected and much smaller. And sharper, like a cartoon that had suddenly come to life. But then it was off, with little stop-start movements, disappearing behind the TV.

This time, though, I'd seen exactly where it had gone. There was a gap where one of the floorboards didn't quite meet the skirting board. I knelt down, holding my breath, waiting to see if it would come out. But it probably knew I was there, curled up like some big cat waiting to pounce.

I was bursting to tell someone. Anyone. So I raced upstairs and knocked on Ned's door. He came out wearing a *what do you want now* look on his face.

"I saw the mouse again," I whispered. "Properly this time. And I've found its hole. It's right behind the TV."

"Great. Now you know where to set the trap. Right outside its front door."

That made it sound so horrible. I suddenly felt as if someone had sucked the air out of me.

"Look, can we talk about this later?" said Ned.

I nodded, but I mustn't have looked very enthusiastic, because he patted me on the head. "Don't worry, big bro'll do it for you."

I hate being patted on the head.

"No, you won't," I snapped. "You'll only make a performance out of it. And I promised Dad I'd do it."

"Oh, well, we can't let Daddy down, can we? Not if we *promised*," he said, going back into his room.

Mum must have heard me moving around the landing because she called, "Michaela, have you done your homework?"

I put my head round the study door. Mum always gets on her computer after Dad's called and she's often there until midnight, which is another reason why she can't get up in the morning.

"I've only got some spellings to look at," I told her. "I'm going to get myself a drink first, though."

I raced down into the kitchen and got a piece of cheese. Then I took the mousetrap out and gave it a good wipe. Then I went into the lounge and closed the door.

I set the trap, being really careful to keep my fingers out of the way. It was a bit of a fiddle to do, but I managed it. Then I placed it right in front of the hole.

I knelt on the carpet for a while, looking at it, which was a big mistake because then I started to think about what Kerry had called it: an instrument of torture. I'm a torturer, I thought, a killer. What if the mouse came out now and got caught in it? What if it got caught later, while I was still awake? Would I be able to hear it from my bedroom, squealing? I felt horrible – and suddenly really tired. It was only half past eight but I just wanted to be in bed.

When I went in to say good night, Mum said, "You look funny. Are you okay?"

"I just feel a bit sick."

Her face went all tight and pinched-looking. She put her hand on my forehead. "You're not going down with something, are you?"

I thought, here we go! If I was ill who'd look after me? She'd have to take time off work and then she'd probably catch whatever I'd got . . . and then she'd have to take even more time off . . . and then she'd get behind with her work . . . and then she'd get stressed . . . and then . . . and then . . . Panic stations! This is how my mum's mind works.

"Don't worry," I said. "I'm fine. I'm just tired. I'm off to bed." I gave her a bright little smile and she seemed to relax. "And don't *you* stay up too late," I told her. "You'll only be tired in the morning."

Honestly, sometimes I sound more like *her* mum.

She gave me a hug. "You are a wonder," she said. "I don't know what I'd do without you, especially with Dad away."

No, I don't either, I thought. But I just kissed the top of her head and went to bed.

I couldn't sleep though. I lay awake for hours thinking about the mouse. I kept imagining I could hear it squealing. In the end I got up and crept downstairs into the lounge. I didn't want to risk waking anyone so I took my torch. I went straight to the trap. It was empty but the cheese was gone. How had it done that?

The house was so quiet it felt quite creepy, which was probably how I managed to hear it: a small scratching sound, coming from behind the newspaper rack. I shone my torch over and saw the mouse peeping out.

It stopped and froze, like a little statue.

I froze too and watched it. I watched its tiny little eyes staring at me. I wondered what I must look like. A great big ogre spying on it?

In that moment I knew there was no way I could kill it.

If it was up to me I'd have let it go back to its hole and live there forever. As far as I was concerned our house was big enough for us and a whole family of mice. But I knew Mum wouldn't agree. And, anyway, even if I let it go, Dad would probably catch it as soon as he came home.

But if I could catch it now, while I had the chance, I didn't need to kill it. I could set it free – somewhere else. *Just get rid of it*, Dad had said.

The Vanishing Mouse Trick

I looked around for something to catch it in.
The wastepaper basket was only inches away.
I leaned sideways, ever so slowly, holding my
breath again. The mouse was watching me. I tried
to keep eye contact with it, sort of hypnotising it,
while my fingers made contact with the basket.
Suddenly the door burst open and my stupid
brother lumbered in.

"Caughtya!" he said.

The mouse took its chance, flying along the top of the skirting board, knocking over the wastepaper basket and disappearing into its hole. Never mind the mouse, I almost jumped out of my skin with fright.

"Now look what you've done," I said.

"Charming! I come down here to help, like a kind-hearted bro'," he said, "and this is the thanks I get?"

"Oh, you were a great help," I snarled.

I crept back upstairs wishing brothers had never been invented.

Chapter Five

I was feeling so tired the next morning I didn't want to get up. But I had to. Someone had to do *droppings patrol*. After that I certainly didn't want any breakfast. But I should have guessed the trouble that would cause.

Mum started clucking round. "Are you still not feeling well, sweetheart? You do look a bit pasty. Perhaps I'd better take your temperature. I hope you're not starting with something."

"Look, I'm fine," I assured her. I said I'd have some toast, just to keep her happy. I took a couple of bites, then, as soon as she turned and started wiping up the crumbs from around the toaster, I stuffed the rest in a piece of kitchen towel.

"Oh, no. Is that another one?" she groaned. Behind the toaster was the one dropping I must

43

have missed. I jumped up quickly and picked it up.

"It's a fly," I said. Neatly dropping it in the bin. "You can tell you haven't got your glasses on."

"Ugh, Michaela, wash your hands this minute. I hope you're right. I hope we've seen the last of that mouse." Then she suddenly thought of something else and all the *what ifs* came pouring out. "What if it was a mouse and what if it got in the cupboards? What if it's contaminated the food? What if we all catch something?"

She went straight to the cupboard under the sink and reached for the bleach, but luckily the clock in the hall chimed. She stood there in the middle of the kitchen, looking so helpless, holding the bleach in one hand and the rubber gloves in the other.

"You go and get ready," I said, taking them off her. "When I get in tonight I'll check the cupboards."

Fortunately she realised this wasn't the time for spring cleaning and went up the stairs, as my brother came down with his nose in a book.

"Just look at this."

He showed me a picture of a magician with a little boy floating in front of him in mid-air. Underneath it said: Ethereal Suspension – Levitation for Beginners.

"It's a con," I said.

He smiled and shook his head. "Oh, ye of little faith."

"It's not real," I told him. "None of it's *real*."

"The mind believes what the eye sees, Micky. It's all a matter of illusion."

"Yeah, yeah," I said. "And some people will believe anything."

He was looking at me with one eyebrow raised – his superior look. It drives me up the wall.

"Have you told Mum you let the mouse get away yet?" he asked.

"Of course I haven't. Anyway it wouldn't have got away if you hadn't interfered."

"Well, don't worry, I won't tell her . . ." he said, smiling.

"Good."

". . . on one condition."

"What are you talking about?"

"I need an assistant. Just to practise with."

"No way! You're not floating me in the air. Forget it."

"Not that, you bozo. I'm not up to advanced stuff like that – not yet. I just need someone to hold things."

"Hold things?"

"Assist me. I'd *like* a tall sexy blonde, really . . ."

"Dream on," I said.

" . . . but you'll do for now. Just half an hour and your secret's safe with me."

"Read my lips. N-O. No!"

"Fair enough. No skin off my nose. I didn't promise Daddyo. I'm not Little-Miss-Perfect-Have-to-Get-it-Right. I'll go and tell her now, shall I?"

46

"What's the point?" I could hear my voice turning to a whine. "You'll only upset her." Not that he cared about that. The trouble was he knew I'd give in rather than cause trouble. He'd trapped me like this before.

"Half an hour," I said. "Not a nanosecond longer."

"Brillo," he said, taking his cards out and making them into a fan. "Take one," he said. "Any card you like."

I gave him such a look. Sometimes my brother goes too far.

When I got to school Kerry was still acting a bit off with me. I knew she was wondering whether I'd done the dirty deed, but she didn't ask and I wasn't going to bring the subject up. Guess who opened his mouth and put his foot right in it, though?

"D'you catch your mouse?" said Max Grimes.

I saw Timmy Winkler's eyes flicker with interest. Anything with blood in it!

"No," I said. "I didn't."

Kerry narrowed her eyes at me.

"Look," I said. "I don't want to kill it. I can't bear to, in fact. But I do need to catch it."

"I can't see why *you* have to do anything," Kerry snapped.

"Well I *could* leave it," I said. There was no point trying to explain to her why it was important to me to do what I'd promised. "But Dad'll only put a trap down the minute he gets back, I can guarantee that."

"Well, I'm just glad I live in a family that loves animals," said Kerry. "They're all God's creatures. It doesn't matter how big or small . . ."

I stopped listening. I'd heard this little lecture enough times before. Kerry and I have been friends ever since the Infants but sometimes she does get on my nerves. But I didn't like the way Max Grimes was staring at her, as if she was some kind of alien species.

"What are you looking at?" I snapped.

"Don't know," he snapped back, "the label's dropped off."

I turned back to the review I was supposed to be writing of my favourite book. I had so many I still couldn't choose, but when Mrs French said, "Anyone finished yet?" I thought, Finished! Blimey! Decision time. And I didn't look up for the next quarter of an hour. It was the longest I'd had my mind off the mouse for the last two days. I was worried I was getting a bit obsessed with it.

By the middle of the afternoon I was no nearer to finding a solution to the problem. I was already feeling pretty irritable and my fight with Max Grimes was the final straw.

We'd just come back from PE. Max hadn't done PE, because he keeps forgetting his PE kit.

Mrs French said she was beginning to think he might be doing it on purpose. I could have told her that a week ago. So he'd stayed in the classroom reading. To tell you the truth I was glad to get a rest from him.

When I came back I just dropped my sweater on the table. And the sleeve happened to fall across the page he was reading. I swear that's all. He threw it right across the room. "Don't mind me," he snarled. "Just treat me like a piece of furniture." And with a sweep of his arm all my books ended up on the floor for the second time that week.

Mrs French came straight over. "Now what's going on?"

I wasn't going to tell her. I stood looking at Max and he sat looking at me. It was like a shoot out in a cowboy film. Mrs French was waiting to see who'd draw first. But neither of us did.

"I'm waiting," she said, in case we hadn't noticed. Everyone else in the class was waiting too and watching us but I didn't care. I wasn't going to crack first.

In the end Mrs French said, "Well, I'll just have to assume then that nothing of importance has happened. That Michaela's sweater flew across the classroom of its own volition and her exercise books decided to take a trip too." The rest of the class giggled, all except me and Max Grimes.

Afterwards we avoided looking at each other. Kerry wouldn't look at me either. Once or twice I caught Timmy Winkler watching me, but when I stared back at him he just ducked his head back to his book and carried on with his drawing.

More bombs, more blood, more flying arms and legs. He's just like my brother: one-track mind.

So I hadn't had a very good day one way and another and I couldn't wait for home time. Then when Mrs French told me to stay behind because she wanted a word with me I couldn't believe my bad luck. I thought, Uh, oh! What's coming now?

Chapter Six

Mrs French started off all sweetness and light, "Michaela, I'm not going to ask you what went on earlier. I'm just going to assume it was some little misunderstanding with Max that you two will sort out between you. I shan't say another word about it . . ."

But I should have known. Teachers never mean what they say. There was plenty more to come yet.

" . . . however I do want to remind you that Max is new here. He's barely had time to make any friends. We all have a responsibility to make him feel welcome in this class. Don't you agree?"

I was too mad to say anything, so I nodded. I couldn't believe *I* was getting it in the neck because *he* lost *his* temper and threw *my* belongings across the room. Life's so unfair!

The Vanishing Mouse Trick

As if she could read my mind, she went on, "Of course, I realise Max can be a bit short-tempered, so perhaps I need to move him on to a table with people who can be a bit more . . . tolerant."

"It's fine," I said. "He doesn't bother me," which wasn't the complete truth. I wanted to tell her I could handle it and she needn't worry about me. But mostly I just wanted to get away, so I said, "Can I go now?"

She smiled and nodded. "I know I can rely on you, Michaela. I've always found you to be one of the most sensible people in the class."

Grrr! *Sensible*. That's another word I hear too often for my liking.

*

I went to the cloakroom to collect my jacket then went out into the playground. Max Grimes was standing waiting for me. I just breathed in and clenched my teeth. But he greeted me as if we were old friends.

"She didn't give you a roasting, did she?"

"No," I said, heading off home. To my horror he followed me.

"There are other kinds of mousetraps, you know."

"Sorry?" What was he on about now?

"You can get humane traps as well. Then you can catch the mouse and set it free. That's what you want to do, isn't it?"

"Oh, right," I said. So that's what the man in the pet shop had meant. I started to walk on. "Well, thanks, anyway." I didn't know what else to say.

"That's okay. I'll see you tomorrow."

Talk about Jekyll and Hyde.

Even though I was home late, by the time Ned got in I'd emptied the food cupboards and was surrounded by a circle of packets and tins. It wasn't long since Dad and I had a clear out and chucked out everything past its sell-by date. So it took me no time really.

In any case there weren't really any gaps in the cupboards where even a mouse could get in. But I wiped the shelves and was about to put everything back when my brother came in whistling.

"A woman's work is never done," he said. I ignored him which is usually the best strategy. "What's this?" he asked.

On the way home I'd been back to see the grumpy man in the pet shop and the new mousetrap was on the kitchen table. "It's a humane mousetrap," I said. "We don't have to kill the poor thing. We just catch it."

"Oh, how very kind and thoughtful," he said. "We won't finish it off cleanly ourselves. We'll evict it instead. We'll throw it out into the wild to be eaten by the first passing cat. Now, that's what I call humane."

"Don't start," I said. I'd heard enough from Kerry without him joining in. "Unless, of course, you've got any better ideas."

"Okay, okay," he said, "keep your wig on. I'll go and let you get on with your chores."

"Good," I said, as he disappeared upstairs. But he was back the next minute.

"Don't forget, Darren'll be round about half six. What're you gonna wear?"

"*Wear?!* And you didn't say anything to me about Darren. You expect me to make a complete idiot of myself in front of him as well?"

"That's about it," he said. "See if you can borrow something sparkly of Mum's."

"In your dreams," I said.

*

Mum looked terrible when she came in. Even more tired than usual. She said work had been a nightmare with so many people at the moment on holiday. She said she was sick of coming home night after night and having to do everything while Dad swanned about in Bristol. I couldn't think what she was talking about. Dad wasn't exactly having a picnic. And as I pointed out I'd just made her a cuppa. (*And* I'd done the cupboards for her, but I didn't mention that. If she'd convinced herself there never was a mouse I didn't want to plant the idea again.)

She said she was out on her feet and she was going to take her tea through into the lounge. She actually fell asleep with it in her hand. Luckily I went in and took it off her before she tipped it all over herself. I didn't put the TV on because I didn't want to disturb her. She looked so peaceful. So I sat opposite her, sort of watching over her. I did wish she wasn't so tired all the time. She didn't sleep for long though. There wasn't much chance with my brother's music blasting away upstairs.

"Sorry, sweetheart," she said, waking up and looking at her cup of tea, which was cold by now.

"I'll make you another one," I said.

When I came back with it, Mum said, "Can you hear that noise?"

Of course I could hear it. But I made out I couldn't.

"There, listen," she said.

It was very faint, but there was a definite rustling. Fortunately Ned's music was thumping away upstairs.

"It's probaby a bird outside," I said, grabbing the remote and flicking the TV on.

"That's not a bird," she said, taking the remote off me and killing the sound. "You don't think it's . . ."

She dropped the remote and pulled her feet up underneath her, as if she expected Minnie to run up her tracksuit bottoms any moment. I grabbed the remote and didn't even let her finish the sentence. "You're getting neurotic, Mum. I've told you, there's no mouse. If there ever was one, it's gone." I turned the sound up and before she could tell me to turn it down, I swiftly changed the subject. "You haven't forgotten Darren's coming tonight? It's just getting a bit late for tea you know."

The Vanishing Mouse Trick

"Oh, yes. I had," she said and got up and headed for the kitchen. I felt mean, because she looked as if she could have done with a bit more of a rest, but I hadn't much choice really.

I wished Dad was here. But he wasn't here, was he? That's why I had to get on with it and catch the mouse. And fast, before Mum actually caught sight of it.

We'd barely finished eating before Dippy Darren arrived. My brother let him in and then put his head round the kitchen door and beckoned me upstairs.

"Time for payback," he said. His face disappeared round the door.

"What's that about?" asked Mum.

"I promised to help him with his magic tricks."

"You don't usually get involved. What's he bribed you with?"

"Nothing," I lied. "I just owe him."

Mum put her arm round me. "Well, don't let him practise on you, sweetie. I don't know how I'd manage if anything happened to you."

I wish. Perhaps he could turn me into a mouse, I thought, then I could escape down a mousehole and come back when it's all over.

The phone rang and I just stopped myself running to get it.

"Don't you want to talk to Dad first?" said Mum, surprised.

"No," I sighed. I had no news for him and I didn't want to have to explain my change of tactics. "Tell him everything's just *fine*."

Chapter Seven

Just when I'd got really pressing things on my mind, I had to spend the longest, most boring half an hour of my entire life with my brother and his brain-dead friend. Yawn, yawn. They seemed more interested in arguing about what they should call themselves than in practising tricks. I offered a few suggestions of my own, but they didn't seem impressed. Ned's favourite was: The Great Nedini and his Dog. Don't even ask! But I'd set my digital watch to make sure they didn't get a second more out of me than we'd agreed. The moment it went off I was out of there!

After half an hour with those two I felt brain-dead myself. I would have liked some intelligent conversation, but Mum was in the bath and I knew better than to disturb her there. Dad calls it her therapy hour. She soaks for so long I'm surprised she doesn't turn into a wrinkled prune.

So I went downstairs to find the new mousetrap to work out how to set it.

This one was like a little plastic tunnel with a lid on one end and a sort of trapdoor on the other. It didn't bite you, like the other one, but it was almost as difficult to set, because the slightest touch caused it to collapse and the trapdoor to close.

You had to put the bait in at one end, prop the door open at the other and hope the mouse would be tempted inside. If it went far enough along the tube its weight made the trap rock forwards and the door close behind it. Hey Presto!

Oh, boy. Now I'm beginning to sound like my brother.

I set the trap up close to the hole and waited for a bit, but I'd watched enough paint drying for one evening. And I could hear Mum calling me to make her a cup of tea.

When I took it up I found her sitting at her computer, in her dressing gown with a towel round her head. She didn't look a bit like a prune, actually. More like a plum.

"Here's your drink," I said.

"What an absolute treasure! The best-cup-of-tea-maker in the world."

My mum's always called me that. She loves her cup of tea but it has to be just right. She drinks Earl Grey and it has to be very, very, very, *very* weak.

This is how you make it. You pour the boiling water into the mug first, then you hold the tea

bag by a corner and sort of
swish it quickly through
the water. If you drop it in
and then have to fish it out
with a spoon it's too late.
You have to pour it away
and start all over again,
because if it actually looks
like a cup of tea, she won't drink it. But I'm an
expert. I make it exactly the way she likes it;
tinted water with a slice of orange.

She spun her chair round and patted her knee.
She sometimes likes me to sit on her lap but it
doesn't work for long because now I'm nearly as
big as she is. She started running her fingers
through my hair, combing it with her fingernails.
I really like that, it makes me feel sleepy.

"How's school going?"

"Same as usual."

"How's Kerry?"

"Same as usual."

"Who else are you sitting with this term?"

"A couple of weirdos."

"What kind of weirdos?"

"Timmy Winkler . . ."

"That can't be his real name."

I nodded and sighed, "It is. He's into blood and guts and not much else. And a dreadful new boy called Max Grimes."

"Why's he dreadful?"

"He's got a seriously bad temper and he keeps knocking my books on to the floor and standing on them."

"Why would he do that?"

"Oh, Mum, how would I know?"

"Well, I suppose it can't be much fun starting a new school part way through the year."

Oh, no. Now I was going to get another lecture about being kind to people. "I know it can't be very nice, but that's no reason to be horrible to everyone."

"Well, you don't know what it's like for him. You've got everything you could possibly want, Michaela. I don't think you always realise how lucky you are."

I thought, *she really believes that*. She thinks because I don't make a fuss I must have everything I want. But I didn't want Dad to be living in

Bristol. And I didn't want her to be working so hard that she was always tired, or asleep, or in her study. And I would have preferred a sister, like Kerry has, instead of a dippy brother who's obsessed with magic tricks.

But there was no point saying any of that. She'd only get upset and then she'd get worried and I'd have to cheer her up again. I sat there feeling her fingers combing through my hair, but I wasn't enjoying it any more.

"I think I'll go to bed," I said.

"Okay, sweetie. Thanks for the tea. You're a little star."

Hmmm, I thought. Well, this is one little star that would like a night off.

Next morning, as soon as I woke, I went downstairs and into the lounge to check the trap before I did *droppings patrol*.

Yes!! The trapdoor was closed! I was so excited, but I picked up the trap really carefully. I didn't want to scare Minnie to death.

I'm not sure why, but ever since I'd seen the mouse I couldn't think of her as *it* any more.

I didn't know whether she was male or female, but I'd decided to call her Minnie anyway.

The trap still felt very light so I couldn't tell whether there was anything in it. I couldn't shake it; such a small creature might die from fright. So I carried it carefully upstairs and tapped on Ned's door.

There was a sort of low growl, the kind of noise that might come out of a prehistoric swamp. "Wodyawan?" I opened the door and went in.

"I need some help," I told him. "I can't tell whether I've caught anything."

He reared up in bed, looking like a particularly bad hair day.

"Oh, for Pete's sake," he said. "Just close the door and disappear."

"Help me first," I pleaded, "then I'll disappear."

"Okay," he said, his eyes starting to glint. "I'll help you, but on one condition: I've seen this great trick in my book . . ."

I slammed his door behind me and left him wallowing in his swamp. My brother is definitely an alien!

I went into my own room and put the trap on my bed. I told myself, I don't need him, I can do this on my own. Just think about it slowly.

I emptied my waste basket and held it out ready in case Minnie made a run for it. With the other hand I gently opened the trapdoor.

I was holding my breath, but now it just came out in a stream, like a balloon going down. The trap was empty. I was so disappointed.

I heard Mum going into the bathroom so I hurried downstairs to the kitchen. Minnie had had a busy night. The evidence was all round the kitchen. I quickly collected it up and then wiped round with Jif and dried the surfaces off with paper towels. I was back upstairs before Mum came out of the bathroom.

I was thinking that Dad would have been pretty pleased with me. But I knew he'd be even more pleased if I managed to get rid of Minnie. And I wasn't looking forward to going to school. I didn't want anyone asking me if I'd caught her yet. I didn't want to have to admit I'd failed again.

Chapter Eight

As it turned out no one even asked me about Minnie. Kerry was just about speaking to me, but not on that subject. Max Grimes wasn't even there.

"I wonder where he is," I said to Kerry after break.

She gave me a sharp look. "Do you know, that's the third time you've said that this morning?"

I could feel myself going red. "I was only wondering."

Considering Max talked all the time we knew nothing about him. We knew nothing about Timmy Winkler either and he's been in the same class as us for years, but he hardly speaks at all, just draws. Although I hate his pictures I can see they're good, full of detail and action. But gruesome.

Kerry was drawing too. Both of them were too busy with their own little projects – hairstyles and violence – to bother with the English comprehension work we'd been set. I decided to get on with it, even though it was boring, since no one was talking to me.

But after lunch when Max Grimes came back from the dentist, he asked me straightaway, "Did you get the trap?"

"Yes," I was glad someone was interested.

"And?"

"It didn't work. She got away."

"She?" said Kerry, butting in. "How d'you know it's a she?"

"I don't know it's a she, but in any case I've called her Minnie." I just dared them all to laugh at me. Luckily for them nobody did.

"What are you baiting it with?" Max asked.

"Cheese."

"You need peanut butter. It's sticky and it's got a strong smell which helps."

"We haven't got any peanut butter." I knew because I'd just cleaned out the cupboards.

"So? Buy some."

It all seemed so much trouble and I was beginning to feel pretty hopeless.

"I've got no money left," I moaned. "I've used it all up buying useless traps and I can't ask my mum because . . ."

"Yeah, yeah, she'll freak if she thinks the mouse is still there. I'd lend it you myself but I'm skint," he said. "What about you lot?"

Timmy Winkler looked up and showed his empty palms.

Kerry gave him a weary look. "You expect *me* to lend *her* money to spend on being cruel to animals. Get a life."

"I'm not being cruel," I said. "That's the whole point. I'm trying to catch her so I can set her free." I knew that sounded cock-eyed, but Kerry of all people should have understood. She was supposed to be my friend.

"Anyway I don't want your money," I told her. "I don't want anything off you." She ignored me and carried on drawing stick-insect women with long stringy hair. I thought, *she* should get a life.

Max raised his eyebrows and gave me a sort of conspiratorial smile. I really couldn't make him out. I was fed up with Kerry but I didn't want him stirring things up between us. Anyway, I thought, he'll have to stop throwing my things about and walking all over them before I smile at *him*.

At the end of the day I waited outside the school gate until Ned came along. I was going to ask him for some money to get some peanut butter, but when I saw him coming down the road in the middle of a gang of boys I was too embarrassed. I walked on ahead, pretending I didn't even know him. But with their great long legs they soon overtook me.

The Vanishing Mouse Trick

Ned slapped me on the back. "Hey, Sis," he said, and roughed up my hair which he knows I hate.

Then he started pulling pound coins from behind my ear, one after another and pocketing them. Or that's what it looked like. It was really the same one over and over again. His stupid friends fell for it, but I knew it was just sleight of hand and I grabbed it and pocketed it myself.

The Vanishing Mouse Trick

So I got the peanut butter after all. I had some on a sandwich when I got in. It was quite nice for a change. Of course when the human vacuum cleaner saw it on the table he ate nearly half a jar spread on Mum's crispbreads. He just whuffed through most of a packet, spilling crumbs all over his library book – *The World's Great Illusionists*!

He was reading about his *main man hero*: Harry Houdini. But Mum's put her foot down about him trying any of those kinds of tricks!

"Listen to this," he said, breaking off eating to read me bits, even though he knows I'm not in the least bit interested. "One time he escaped from the belly of a whale! He was lowered head first into a tank of water and padlocked inside. And he still got out in two minutes. Can you believe that?"

"No," I said. "Even if I'd *been there* I wouldn't have believed it."

He looked at me pityingly. "So young and so cynical."

As soon as Ned turned back to his book I did a quick vanishing trick of my own, taking the jar of peanut butter with me. Otherwise there'd have been none left for Minnie.

The Vanishing Mouse Trick

*

The phone went at seven and I thought I'd
better talk to Dad or Mum
would suspect something was
wrong.

"Hi, Micks. How's tricks?"

"Okay."

"Are you sure? You
don't sound okay."

"Dad, when are you
coming home?"

"I told you. At the weekend. I shall need to
come back here next week, but the job's almost
finished. How's the little
problem?"

"I haven't caught her yet.
But I'm working on it."

"Just keep her out of
Mum's way, that's the
main thing. As long as
she doesn't see her."

"I don't know why she's so
scared of a little mouse," I grumbled. "Minnie
wouldn't hurt a fly."

"Oh, we're on first name terms, are we?"

"She's dead . . . cute, Dad, really." I couldn't believe I'd said that.

"Who's cute?" said Mum, coming up behind me.

"No one," I said. "A girl at school's got a puppy, that's all."

I handed over the phone. Another little lie. I was getting too good at them.

Grandma rang later that night. She wanted to know all about school. I made her laugh telling her about the people on my table.

"I'm sure you keep them in order, Michaela," she said.

"I try, Grandma."

"Perhaps you need some new friends. Someone you've got more in common with. Someone with a bit of get up and go." Grandma was very keen on *get up and go*.

I was beginning to think she was right about friends. I was tempted to confide in her about my problems with Minnie too, but Mum came along and took the phone off me.

The Vanishing Mouse Trick

While she was safely occupied – she and
Grandma talk for hours once they get started –
I sneaked off and set the trap with a big blob of
peanut butter. I left it hidden behind the TV and
went upstairs to read in bed.

Later on Mum came in to turn off my light.

"Are you all right, sweetie? You're very quiet
tonight."

I don't know what she means when she says
that; I'm always quiet.

"Yeah. I'm fine. Mum, can I have a pet?" I said, throwing her off the scent.

She blinked in surprise. Her forehead wrinkled up. Mum's even less into animals than I am, she thinks they're little germ factories. "I suppose we could talk about it, when Dad comes home," she sighed, "if you *really* want one. Do you want one?"

"Probably not," I said. "Just testing. Perhaps I'll have a clarinet instead."

Mum shook her head and smiled at me. "You are a strange girl."

"I know," I said. "I wonder who I take after?"

Chapter Nine

When my alarm went off, I had to force myself to get out of bed. I know my family are all mad, but sometimes I think I'm the maddest! I crept downstairs to check the trap. Nothing, again!

It seemed to have moved a little way from where I'd set it, but it was definitely empty. So what did that mean? Perhaps Minnie didn't like peanut butter! I was getting mad now. I really wanted to show Dad I could do this but I was running out of time. I only had two chances left: today, while I was at school, or tonight, while I was in bed.

I left the trap set up, positioned carefully near the hole. Then I went into the kitchen and cleared up even more droppings than ever.

It looked as if Minnie had had all her friends in for a party. Then I headed back upstairs to get dressed.

When I came down my brother was leaning against the sink eating cold baked beans from the tin. He knows Mum hates it and it really winds me up. But I decided to ignore him and got myself a yoghurt out of the fridge.

"D'you remember that bloke in the paper . . ." he said between mouthfuls " . . . found a dead mouse in a tin of beans . . . sued the company for thousands of pounds . . . said it had traumatised him?" I was still ignoring him, but he just kept on. "Hey, Pud, d'you remember?"

In the end I turned round and saw the joke. Or at least his twisted idea of a joke. A long piece of string was hanging from the corner of his mouth.

"You're not funny," I said.

"Wha'dyamean," he grunted, trying to look innocent. "Oh, this?" Then he started to pull on it. In the end he had to put the tin down and use both hands because it kept coming and coming and coming, as if he'd swallowed a whole ball of string.

"You're so gross," I said, but I couldn't help laughing.

"What's he up to now?" said Mum in a weary voice as she came into the kitchen. But he'd already scooped up the string and pocketed the evidence. I shook my head, "Don't even ask." *I* wasn't going to spill the beans!

Then she saw the tin. "Oh, Ned, why can't you eat them off a plate like any civilised human being?"

"I'm perfectly civilised," said my brother, grinning. Then he put his hand over his mouth and did a huge burp. Suddenly an egg popped out. Then another, and another.

Mum and I just looked at each other and burst out laughing.

"What's he like?" said Mum.

"Rather *egg-centric*," I said.

Then we couldn't stop giggling. All of us. It was nice. I haven't seen Mum laugh like that in ages.

*

I was tempted to tell them at school about Ned's joke but I knew Kerry wouldn't find it funny. And I didn't want to fight with her any more so I decided not to mention the subject, but I should have known who would. It was the first thing Max said: "Any luck last night?"

"Not that again," Kerry groaned.

I didn't say anything, I just shook my head and kept my eyes down.

"Did you try peanut butter, like I said?"

"Ye-e-s." I wished he'd just leave it alone. But he wasn't going to.

"Where are you putting the trap?"

"Outside her hole, of course."

"How do you know it's her hole?" said Kerry, butting in again.

"Because I saw her go into it."

"She might have lots of different holes," said Max.

Hmmm, I hadn't thought of that.

"Well, perhaps you'll be lucky tonight," he said.

"If I'm not that's my last chance before Dad comes home."

"I don't get it," said Max. "Why's that so important?"

I wasn't going to bother trying to explain to him, but Kerry butted in again.

"Micky likes to prove things. She thinks she's Superwoman."

I didn't say anything. I didn't need to. When people say things like that it just makes me more determined than ever.

For the rest of the morning I kept my head down and pretended to be completely absorbed in my work. Obviously I wasn't, but I'm quite a good actress if I say so myself.

Nothing else much happened during the day. It was just the usual. Then I started to get a headache. I think it was partly because I was feeling so tired. I wanted to put my head down and cool my face on the table. Nearly everything we had to do was in pairs and Kerry and I were really crunchy with each other. I thought again about what Grandma had said about finding a new friend.

But it wasn't that easy. When I looked around the classroom I couldn't see any likely candidates.

The Vanishing Mouse Trick

It might have been easier if I was into netball, which I'm not. Or in the choir. Or the orchestra. That's why I'd asked Mum about a clarinet. I wasn't really interested, but it did cross my mind as a possibility, if I got desperate.

I was in a five star bad mood by the time I got home that night. And when I saw the trap still empty it didn't help a bit. As if that wasn't enough Ned started to bug me again about helping him with his silly magic tricks. I was even glad when Darren came round, at least it gave me some peace.

It was nearly half past eight before I realised Dad hadn't rung. I'd got the downstairs to myself because Mum was in the bath and Ned and Darren were in his bedroom. It was lovely and quiet, and I was watching what Mum calls mindless telly: soaps and quiz shows. Until my brother's face appeared round the door.

"Pud, have you seen the ball of string?"

I reminded him he'd eaten it that morning.

"Oh, yes. By the way can I just ask you . . ."

I didn't even look round. "The answer's no."

"You don't know the question yet."

"I can guess. And the answer's still no."

"I just wanted your opinion."

"On what?"

He did a sort of drumroll. "Introducing . . . The Great Nedini and Dario!" I looked at him as if he was talking Chinese. "Our stage names, dummy."

I suggested Noddy and Big Ears would be better.

"Thanks a bunch," he said, pulling a bouquet of flowers out of his sleeve and throwing it to me. "Good joke, eh?"

I caught it and threw it back. "Don't ring us, we'll ring you." I turned back to the TV and muttered to myself, "I am so glad I'm not a boy."

But Ned heard me and said, "Perhaps, if you were, you might have had some success by now with The Great Mouse Hunt." He went back upstairs and left me sitting there simmering like a pan of soup getting near to the boil.

Chapter Ten

When my programme finished I went upstairs to check Mum hadn't fallen asleep in the bath. It wouldn't be the first time. But I found her sitting on the side of the bath, reading a magazine, waiting for the colour she'd put on her hair to work.

"What's the time?" she asked.

I told her, "Twenty to nine."

"Already?" She grabbed the shower head and started to rinse it off. "It was only meant to be left on five minutes. I dread to think what colour it'll be."

When she surfaced I said, "Dad hasn't rung yet and it's nearly nine. D'you think he's all right?"

"Oh, sorry, I forgot to tell you. He's working late, but he'll be here tomorrow, by the time you get in from school. We'll have a nice meal to celebrate. And Darren's coming."

"Why's *he* coming?" I said.

"They want to show us some of the tricks they've been practising."

"Oh, great! Watching more paint dry."

"It'll be fun," said Mum. "Ned might do the egg trick again."

But I wasn't in the mood for jokes. I didn't want Darren here. But most of all I didn't want to have to tell Dad I still hadn't caught the mouse.

Mum went into her bedroom to dry her hair.

I felt too tired and grumpy to do anything, but I made myself go downstairs to set the trap, knowing this would be my last chance.

I stopped to think about what Max had said, about Minnie having different holes. Perhaps I should leave the trap somewhere different. The one thing I knew for sure was that at night, when we were all in bed, Minnie's favourite place seemed to be the kitchen. At least that's where the droppings were. Perhaps I should leave the trap there, on the work surface.

But how could I do that, without Mum finding it? She often doesn't go to bed until midnight and she usually comes down to the kitchen first to make herself a mug of camomile tea. Well, I'd just have to try to stay awake and come down after she'd gone to bed.

I lay in bed reading, but my eyes wouldn't stay open and I kept dropping my book. I felt like Mum – *exhausted*. When I heard Ned seeing Darren out and locking up, I called to him.

He came in and sat on my bed. "What's up, Pud? Can't you get to sleep?"

"I can't stay awake is the problem. Ned, will you do me a favour?"

"Depends."

I knew this was going to cost me but I really needed his help. As I'd expected he started up again about his stupid tricks.

But this time I was too tired to argue. In the end I said, "All right. *If* we manage to catch her."

He looked like someone who'd won the lottery. "Fantabuloso!" he said, rubbing his hands together.

"Don't get too excited," I told him.

I was pretty sure he wouldn't have any more luck than I'd had. And if he did, well, I'd have to find some way to wriggle out of it. Houdini-style!

I fished under my bed and handed him the trap and the peanut butter.

"I wondered where that had gone," he said.

He tucked me in and turned off my light. "You get a good night's sleep, Little Pudding, and leave everything to me. Big Bro'll catch that mouse for you." My eyes were already closing. Sometimes brothers aren't such a bad idea.

The Vanishing Mouse Trick

*

The next morning, when my alarm went off,
I nearly turned over and went back to sleep. Oh,
but it was a good job I didn't. I dragged myself
out of bed, slid my feet into my slippers and
shuffled down to the kitchen. I wasn't sure the
trap would have been set. You can't always trust
my brother.

But when I saw it sitting on the worktop all
closed up, I just knew Minnie was inside it. The
minute I picked it up I felt her scurry from one
end to the other. I was almost shaking. Not
because I was scared of her, but scared I might
hurt her. I wondered how long she'd been in
there. It must have been hours already.

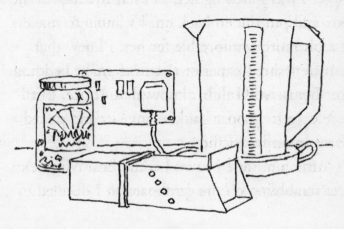

My mind was suddenly spinning. How much air would such a tiny creature need? She was alive so far, but how soon before she would run out? I needed to get her out of there – and quickly.

I raced upstairs to my bedroom and pulled out the shoebox I'd been keeping my new trainers in. I stabbed some holes in each end of the box with a pair of scissors. Then I laid the trap inside and slowly opened the trapdoor.

I had to wait a minute or two before a tiny nose peeped out, then shot back inside. I sat on my bed holding the box lid, ready to pop it on if she tried to escape. At the moment there was no sign of that.

I think Minnie was too frightened to come out while I was watching her, so I left the trap in the box and put the lid back on. I wanted to make it a bit more comfortable for her. I knew that hamsters shred paper or tissues to make bedding for themselves; I didn't know about mice. But I tore up a few paper hankies anyway and poked them in under the lid.

After a minute or two I could hear Minnie's feet scrabbling on the cardboard so I decided to

risk a peep. I lifted the lid back, just a fraction, and there she was looking back at me.

She froze like a little statue, just the way she had the other night when I caught her behind the paper rack. I had that same feeling that I was a horrible ogre spying on her, but I couldn't stop myself. She was so . . . perfect.

When I lifted the lid back for a better view, she shot into the trap. It must have felt safer, out of view of a great big giant like me.

Just then I heard Mum moving around the landing. I put the lid back on the box, weighted it down with my trainers and slid it under my bed. I started to get dressed for school and then it hit me. All in a rush.

What was I going to do with her now? I couldn't leave her here in the box all day. How could I be sure she wouldn't die of lack of air?

I heard Mum go into Ned's bedroom and say, "Come on, get up. It's Friday. Pick your clothes up before Mrs Headley comes. Come on. Chop, chop!"

Then she opened my bedroom door and threw a clean set of bedding on to the end of my bed.

"Try and tidy round a bit, sweetie."

That settled it. I definitely couldn't leave Minnie for the cleaning lady to find. All the time I was changing my bed my mind was racing. Perhaps I could sneak down now to the end of the garden and leave Minnie there. But if I did she'd probably have found her way back into the house by the time I got home from school.

No, I needed to find her a proper home, far enough away so she wouldn't come back. Ned was right; I'd evicted her from her own home and the least I could do was find her another one.

There was nothing else for it. I'd have to take her to school with me.

Chapter Eleven

With all the practice I'd had telling little white lies, I thought I'd have no trouble keeping Minnie a secret. But when I carried my duffle bag into school I felt as if everyone knew what I'd got inside it. I felt as if my face had *Mousecatcher* written all over it in highlighter pen.

I suppose it would have been safer to have left Minnie in my bag in the cloakroom. But I needed to keep my eye on her.

If I almost emptied my drawer and put my books on my table, I was pretty sure the box would fit in. I slid it out of my bag and lifted a corner of the lid and peeped inside. Minnie shot back into the trap. I flapped the box lid a few times to give her some fresh air. Suddenly I heard my name.

"Michaela, could you sit down, please? I'm waiting to start the register."

I pushed the box into my drawer and closed it so fast I almost trapped my fingers in it. Then I hurried back to my place. My face was on fire and I felt as if everyone was watching me.

Max Grimes was definitely watching me – and grinning. He doesn't miss a thing! "What you got in the box?"

"Nothing. Crayons and stuff."

"Let's borrow them," said Kerry, drawing as usual.

"They're new. I'm not allowed to lend them," I said, going even redder. I don't think I've ever said anything so stupid in my life.

Kerry looked at me as if I was either not quite well or up to something. "Suit yourself," she said.

But I could tell Max Grimes wasn't fooled. "You must have a *lot* of crayons."

I pretended I hadn't heard and got on with my work. It was difficult to keep finding excuses to go over to my drawer. But, whenever I could, I lifted the lid to let in a bit more air for Minnie.

I was checking my watch every ten minutes; I couldn't wait for lunchtime to get her out of the classroom. But before then disaster struck.

The whole class had been really noisy all morning, as if everyone knew something was going on. Mrs French was getting seriously fed up with us.

"I won't put up with another minute of this dreadful noise. I've asked you several times to work more quietly. Since you can't manage that, you can spend the rest of the lesson in silence. Take out your reading books and we'll have silent reading until the bell."

It was only then that I realised how much noise Minnie must have been making. Now it was so quiet you could have heard a pin drop – or a mouse scratch!

At first I hoped I was imagining it. But I wasn't. I hoped I was the only one who could hear it. But I wasn't. Mrs French looked up and glanced round the room. "Can anyone else hear that?" she said, frowning.

Everyone stopped reading and looked up. Fortunately the noise stopped too. I held my breath and prayed that Minnie had decided to have a snooze. No such luck. Mrs French got up from her chair.

Oh, no, I thought. Please don't. I must have gone the colour of strawberry jam. Max Grimes was staring at me. Inside I was in complete panic. And then chaos broke out.

Max picked up his ruler and poked Kerry really hard.

"Stop that!" he said.

"What! What are you talking about?" she squealed.

"That noise. It's getting on my nerves." He poked her again. "Stop it, or else."

"But I'm not doing anything!" Kerry wailed.

In a moment Mrs French was standing by our table.

"He keeps poking me," Kerry wailed again. "For nothing."

"What's going on, Max? Explain yourself," she said.

But Max didn't bother. He just started sweeping Kerry's things off the table. Mrs French grabbed him by the shoulder. "Max, this is outrageous! Outside Mrs Whitham's room this minute!"

And to make sure he got there she took him herself.

Everyone was either staring at Kerry or trying to cheer her up. But I had to grab my chance while I'd got it. I hurried over to my drawer and lifted the box lid. When Minnie shot into the trap I closed the trapdoor on her.

"It's only for half an hour," I whispered to her, "while I have my dinner."

Then Mrs French was back and we all had to sit in *absolute* silence for the last five minutes.

I sneaked a look at Kerry. She was still red-eyed and looking very sorry for herself. I felt sorry for her too. But what could I say? And it had been in a good cause.

What I kept asking myself, though, was why Max had got himself into mega-trouble just to help me? I couldn't understand. It was a complete mystery.

Even though I felt bad about Kerry, at lunchtime I avoided her and headed for the end of the football field. I'd got Minnie in my bag. No matter how carefully I carried it, the box kept banging against my leg and I was worried I was giving her a bumpy ride.

I looked back over my shoulder a couple of times and nearly died when I saw Max trying to catch up with me. I was tempted to try and hide from him too, but that seemed mean after the way he'd helped me. I waited until he was almost up to me.

"Come on. Hurry up," I said. "I haven't got long."

"Where are you going?"

"As far away as I can."

When I reached the end of the field I sat down on the grass. I didn't want to open my bag at first. I still wasn't completely sure I could trust him.

"You've got the mouse in there, haven't you?" he said.

I couldn't lie. "I need to give her some air."

I took the box out of my bag and Max dropped down next to me. I lifted the lid, then took the end off the trap to see if Minnie would come out. We had to be really patient. It seemed like hours before she stuck out her nose.

"Magic," Max whispered. And it was.

It was really exciting having her outside. It was quite sunny so I balanced the lid on top of the box until three-quarters of it was in shade. Minnie came out very slowly, checking it was safe. We sat and watched her clean her whiskers. But the moment I reached into my pocket to get her one of the bits of cheese I'd brought, she shot back into the trap.

I put a couple of little scraps of cheese right by the entrance and she stuck out her head and sniffed one suspiciously. Then she grabbed it and disappeared inside again.

"What are you going to do with her?" Max asked.

"I've got to find her a new home."

"Why can't you let her go here?"

"She's a *house mouse*," I said.

"Mmmm," he agreed. "Anyway she might head for the school building, then old Parkie would get her." Parkie was the caretaker. "Or his cat."

"Oh, don't," I said.

"You need a building where there aren't any people . . ."

"Or cats!" I said. "And it mustn't be far away. I can't be late home today."

"I know the place," he said. "There's some allotments behind our house. One or two of them have got sheds. There'd be lots of things to eat there. I could show you after school."

"Okay," I nodded. Then we sat without talking for a bit – hoping Minnie would come out again, but I think the sun was too bright for her.

"Thanks for creating a diversion this morning," I said. "What happened?"

He grinned. "Just got an earwigging. I had to apologise to Mrs French and promise I'd try to keep my temper. They keep giving me extra chances 'cos I'm still new to the school, but I think I'd better watch it from now on."

"I feel a bit sorry for Kerry," I told him.

"She'll understand when we tell her."

"I don't think she will."

"Well, we couldn't have managed it without her, could we?"

I suddenly noticed that people were heading back into school. I closed the trapdoor and slipped the box back in my bag.

The Vanishing Mouse Trick

We walked back into school together and while I put the shoebox into my drawer Max went over and tried to make his peace with Kerry. I thought, rather him than me!

Thank goodness things were easier in the afternoon. We had art and PE. Both gave me more chance to move around. Max didn't do PE, as usual. I don't think he'll get away with that for much longer either! Kerry seemed to have forgiven Max, but she was still feeling sorry for herself so Mrs French said she could be excused too. And if she could trust the two of them not to fall out they could stay in the classroom.

They had the room to themselves for nearly an hour and when I came back from the hall they were all pally-ally. And they had Minnie's box out on the table! I nearly blew a fuse, but Max calmly put a pile of books on top of it.

"Keep your hair on," he said. "She's safe."

"She's so cute, isn't she," Kerry said to him.

I didn't like the way they were behaving as if Minnie was *their* mouse. And when they tried to tell me she'd almost taken some cheese from them, I felt really furious.

Thank goodness it was almost home time.

"Kerry's coming with us after school," Max announced. "She knows an even better place we can take her."

"It used to be a corner shop but it's been boarded up for ages."

"Where is it?" I asked.

"Don't worry, we'll show you," said Kerry, all bossy and in charge.

I wasn't sure I wanted those two taking over, but I bit my tongue and said nothing. I was desperately short of time. And I had to face it, I needed their help.

Chapter Twelve

When we left school there were still lots of kids and a few mums and dads drifting down the road, so we walked really slowly, trying to look cool and laid back, as if we were going nowhere in particular. So it was a horrible shock when Ned suddenly barged out of the door of the mini-market, carrying two enormous cardboard boxes.

"Hi, Pud," he said. He waved the boxes at me. "Got the props!"

"You go on," I said. "I'll be home later."

But suddenly he wasn't in such a hurry, as if he knew I was trying to get rid of him. He put the boxes down and looked Max and Kerry up and down. Then he did the thing I always dread. He started on his tricks. He patted Kerry on the head, put his hand behind her ear and pulled out an egg.

"Cool trick," said Max, which is the worst thing you can say to my brother.

"Don't encourage him," I groaned.

But, too late. He started pulling playing cards out of Max's pocket. I stood there rolling my eyes just wanting the pavement to open up and swallow me.

"What are the boxes for?" Max asked. But before Ned could answer I said, "Look, we've got to go." And I dragged them with me up the next side street.

"Have you forgotten Daddyo's coming home?" Ned called after us.

"I'll be back," I called. "Soon!"

"I think your brother's great," said Kerry.

"You can have him, as a present."

"What's wrong with him?" Max asked.

"Don't get me started."

When we came to Kerry's corner shop I had to admit it was perfect. There was no one in sight but, if anyone did come along, there was an alleyway down the side. The windows and the door were boarded up, but the door had been vandalised and the bottom was badly splintered, with gaps just the right size for Minnie to get through.

I put my bag on the floor, took out the box and lifted the lid. Then I took the trap out and slipped the end off.

I suddenly felt awkward now it was time to say goodbye to Minnie. Part of me wanted to get it over quickly before anyone came past and asked us what we were up to. Part of me just wanted to put her back in the box and take her home with me. But I knew I couldn't do that and it felt harder, knowing Kerry and Max were watching me.

"Aren't you even going to say goodbye to her?" asked Kerry, as if I was this really heartless kind of person, which is actually how I felt.

"Give me a chance," I snapped at her.

I already told you, I'm not really an animal person. It wasn't as if Minnie was a pet or anything. But I had got sort of attached to her. And it did seem odd, posting her like a letter under a door and walking away. The truth is, I didn't know how to say goodbye with those two watching me.

The Vanishing Mouse Trick

But time was running out. I peeped inside the trap and put my mouth close to the opening. "Good luck, Minnie," I whispered. "You're on your own now."

Then I put the open end of the trap against the bottom of the door. I tapped it to encourage her to come out. We waited for a minute or two but nothing happened. So I tilted it, just slightly, to help her on her way. I didn't want to tip her out exactly, just give her a helping hand. But she still wouldn't budge.

"Come on, Minnie," I said. "Don't mess me about."

"She's probably scared," said Kerry. As if I didn't already know that.

"Just be patient," said Max.

"I haven't time to be patient," I snapped, jiggling the trap. "I'm already late."

"She'll have to come out some time," said Kerry.

But why would she? Perhaps she was completely attached to the trap. Perhaps she'd got so used to it she was starting to think it was her home.

"Why don't you push the trap through as well," Kerry suggested. "Then she can come out when she's good and ready."

I thought about that, and I would have done it, but the gap wasn't quite big enough. I looked at my watch again. I had wanted to be home by now. I was already feeling frantic before Max dropped his bombshell.

"Anyway you'll need that trap again."

"What for?" I asked him.

"To catch the rest."

I turned round and stared. " What do you mean – *rest*?"

"Well, you don't just get one mouse," he laughed. "Mice don't live on their own. When we had ours we caught six altogether."

"Six!" I almost screamed. "Six!!!"

"I don't think you should have told her that," said Kerry.

I had to go through this six times?! No way. I sat down on the floor in a heap, ready to cry. The trap slid away from me and out trotted Minnie. She paused for a fraction of a second and then made a quick dash. Not under the door as we'd intended, but along the doorsill and towards the dustbin.

"Catch her!" I shrieked. Kerry headed after her. Minnie froze for a second, just giving Kerry time to cut her off before she disappeared down the alley.

So Minnie turned and darted back the way she'd come. But Max was ready and stuck out his foot to stop her heading in the other direction. I was on my knees, holding the trap out in case she came towards me. With all exits blocked she finally ducked under the door and disappeared from sight. I could hardly believe we'd done it.

The Vanishing Mouse Trick

"Da-daaa!" I stuck my hands out hoping for some applause. "Micky's Amazing Vanishing Mouse Trick!"

Max and Kerry started cheering too.

"Do you think she'll stay in there now?" I said.

"Who knows," said Max, "but we've done our best."

"And saved another poor creature from extinction," said Kerry.

Well, hardly extinction, I was about to say, but I didn't want to argue, not now. Instead I said, "Thanks. I couldn't have done it on my own."

It seemed hard then just to walk off and leave them, but I had to.

"I've got to go. I'm late already."

"We'll see you on Monday, then," said Max.

"You might," I said. "Or not. It all depends on my stupid brother."

As I turned and set off running, I heard Max say to Kerry, "She's seriously weird, isn't she?"

"Tell me about it," said Kerry. "She's been like that since the Infants."

I ran all the way home, stopping once or twice to catch my breath.

My bag, with the empty box in it, was banging against my leg. But this time it didn't matter a bit. I felt in a better mood than I'd done for ages.

Max Grimes was okay, once you got to know him. And Kerry wasn't a bad friend. She'd certainly been there in the end when I needed her.

From the end of our street I could see Dad's car parked outside the house and I felt like cheering. I did the last stretch at a jog and burst through the door squealing, "Dad! Dad! Dad!" I sounded like a five-year-old.

Dad was in the kitchen washing up. "Where's the fire?"

I threw myself on to him and we had a great big bear hug. I was so pleased to have him home I almost started crying, but Ned was there and I'd never have heard the end of that.

Mum wasn't home yet, so Dad asked straight-away, "What's the news?" He raised one eyebrow. "Mission accomplished?"

"Yeah," I said. "Invader successfully repelled."

"Really?" said Dad, as if he was genuinely surprised. "You got rid of it? All on your own?"

I looked over at Ned, who was waiting, grinning, like the cat that had *almost* got the cream.

"Not exactly on my own," I said. "Ned helped a bit."

"Well, good for you," said Dad. "That's really fantastic. You are two pretty cool kids." Ned and I grinned at each other. "And teamwork's usually the best approach. So I can rely on you next time, can I? Because you know, mice don't usually come in ones."

"I *know* that," I said. I didn't even want to think about how big Minnie's family might be. But I still had the trap, if we needed it.

Suddenly we heard Mum's key in the door.

"I think we'll keep this quiet," whispered Dad. "Just the three of us. Our little secret."

We all smiled like conspirators. Then Ned said, "Okay by me, but you'll have to excuse us, Daddyo. *We* have a little secret of our own, don't we, Sis?" And he left the room, beckoning me to follow.

"What's that about?" asked Dad.

"Oh, just something I promised in a moment of weakness," I said, pretending to strangle myself.

When Mum came in, she and Dad had a big hug that went on for ages.

"Let me in," I said, elbowing my way between them. Then we all started dancing round the

kitchen, like a sandwich, with me as the filling.
It was great to feel like a family again. But after a
bit Mum and Dad started doing that smoochy
stuff and I thought, Uh oh, I'm out of here.

I thought I might as well go upstairs and do what a girl's gotta do. After all, a promise is a promise, even when it's made to the most irritating brother on the entire planet. I just hoped that for once he knew what he was doing.

Before I went I thought I'd just check out what was for tea. Dad opened the oven to show me, while Mum went to find a bottle of wine.

Lasagna! Dad's speciality. There was a huge dish of it covered with cheese which was bubbling up nicely and smelling heavenly. I started drooling.

"I'm so hungry," I whined.

"Well, it won't be long," Dad laughed.

"Can't I have mine now?" I begged. "Just in case it all goes horribly wrong."

"In case *what* goes horribly wrong?" said Mum.

"Ned's latest hair-brained scheme."

"What's that?" Dad looked suspicious.

"The Vanishing Micky Trick. Now you see her," I said, disappearing round the door. "Now you don't." Quite an exit, if I say so myself!

HAMISH
Climbing Father's Mountain

W.J. Corbett

Hamish is a mountain goat. All his friends are mountain goats. The only trouble is – Hamish is *terrified* of climbing mountains. Every day his friends clatter off to seek adventure in the high hills, and every day Hamish makes more excuses to stay behind in the comfort of his heathery bed.

Until one day, Hamish hears a cry for help – and only he can save the day . . .

Another Story Book from Hodder Children's Books

WILLIAM AND THE WOLVES

Kathryn Cave

William's little sister Mary has lots of annoying habits, but the worst is her invention of an imaginary friend. Not just any old imaginary friend, but a *lamb*. The rest of William's family think Mary is adorable, and humour her, but William is irritated.

Now *he's* invented some imaginary friends. Only there are six of them. And they're wolves. It looks like Lamb could be in for a shock . . .

h **HODDER** Another Story Book from Hodder Children's Books

DARK AT THE FOOT OF THE STAIRS

Eileen Moore

Spiders! Like them or loathe them – every house has got them. But Tommy Cotton's spider is rather unusual . . .

It's much much bigger than your average creepy-crawly, and it could be lurking about anywhere.

It likes bananas, frogs, and the dark at the foot of Grandma Cotton's stairs . . .

h HODDER

Another Story Book from Hodder Children's Books

IMOGEN AND THE ARK

William Mayne

When Imogen sees the Ark in the toyshop she knows it has to belong to her.

But overnight the shop burns down. Could any toys survive that? The fire engine's hoses cause a flood, but what else is an Ark built for?

How far does the flood reach, what lives in it, what storms rage? Only Imogen sees the terrors of the Ark's journey. Only Imogen sees its long journey home again with its living cargo . . . where she is ready and waiting.

Another Story Book from Hodder Children's Books

A Dog of my Own

Alan Brown

All Tom ever wanted was a dog of his own. And when trouble strikes, his dream comes true and George bounds into his life.

This wild puppy arrives just when Tom needs him the most, and Tom will do anything to keep him . . .